3-14

Little Nelly's
Big Book

For my own beloved Mouse, who isn't one
—P. G.

For my beautiful daughter, Alice, who is also not a mouse
—A. R.

First published in Great Britain in January 2012 by Bloomsbury Publishing Plc
Published in the United States of America in July 2012
by Bloomsbury Books for Young Readers
www.bloomsburykids.com

For information about permission to reproduce selections from this book, write to
Permissions, Bloomsbury BFYR, 175 Fifth Avenue, New York, New York 10010

Library of Congress Cataloging-in-Publication Data
available upon request
ISBN 978-1-59990-779-6

Art created digitally
Typeset in Caslame
Book design by Claire Jones

Printed in China by C&C Offset Printing Co., Ltd., Shenzhen, Guangdong
2   4   6   8   10   9   7   5   3

Little Nelly's Big Book

Pippa
Goodhart

ILLUSTRATED BY
Andy Rowland

BLOOMSBURY

NEW YORK LONDON NEW DELHI SYDNEY

Little Nelly looked in a book
and found out . . .

. . . that she was **a mouse.**

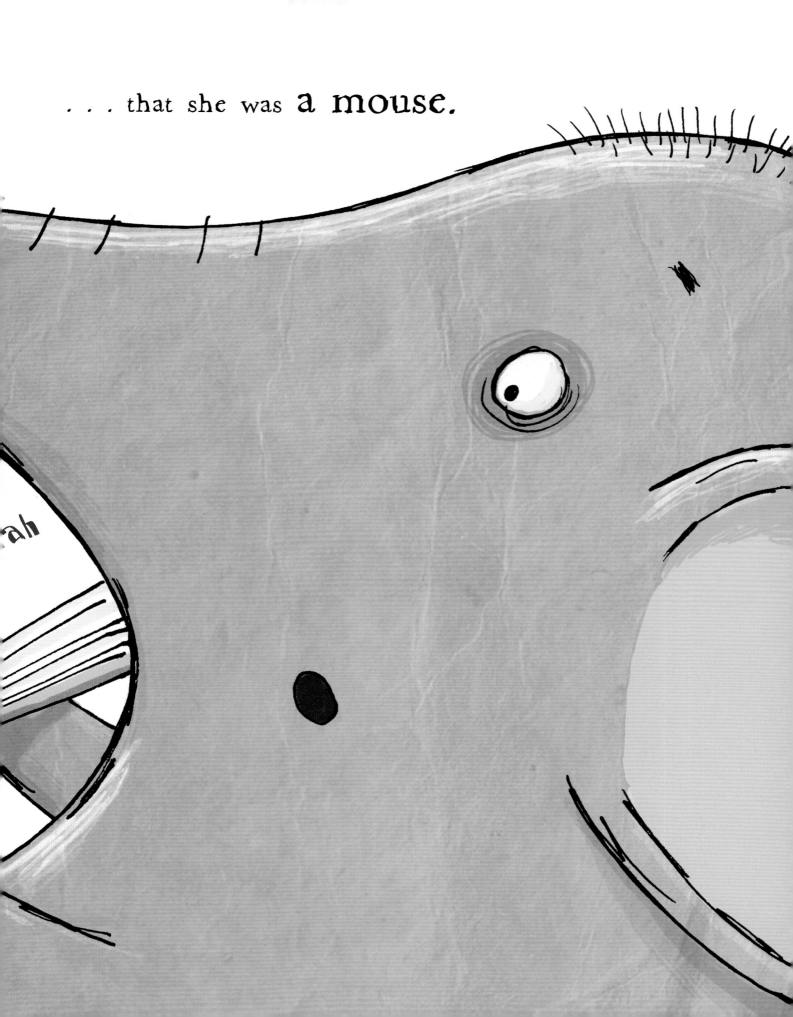

After such a big discovery, Little Nelly was tired.

"I need somewhere to sleep," she said.

Little Nelly looked
in the book again,
and she read . . .

Mice have homes
behind holes in
the wall.
They like to
chew

blah

ah blah

ah blah

blah blah

ah blah blah

So Little Nelly went home.

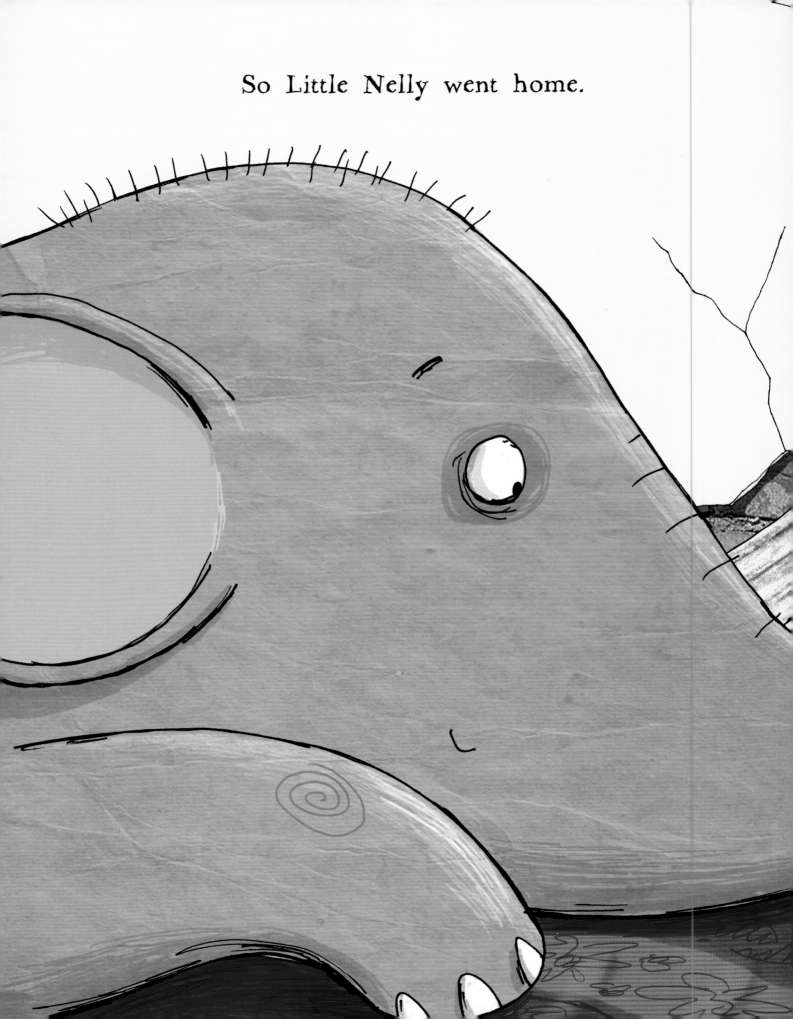

"Hello," said Little Nelly. "I'm a new mouse for your house."

"Um, you're kind of a big mouse," said Micky.

"I'm not!" said Little Nelly.
"If I'm a big mouse, why am I
called Little Nelly?"

"I don't think you're a
mouse at all," said Micky.

"I am!" said Little Nelly.

"I AM! I looked
in a book, and it
says that I am."

"Don't worry about what anybody says, Little Nelly," said Granny Mouse. "You're very welcome here. We'll take care of you."

And they did.

Little Nelly fit in very well.

But even though
the other mice
were kind to her,

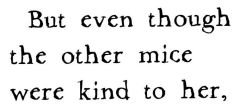

Little Nelly
sometimes
felt she was
different.

And she did get awfully hungry.

Granny Mouse saw how things were, and she had an idea.

"Little Nelly," she said, "I've been asking around, and I found out that there are other mice like you. Most of them live far away, but some live in a zoo nearby."

"Really?" said Little Nelly. "Can we go and see them, please?"

"Of course," said Granny Mouse.

Big
Book
OF

So they all set off for the zoo.

"**Wow!** Look at all the zoo mice," said Micky. "They're just like you, Little Nelly, only bigger!"

"I told you I was little!" said Little Nelly.

The zoo mice were kind and nice to the visiting mice. There were big helpings of food (and other stuff).

"Would you like to live here with us?"
the zoo mice asked Little Nelly.
"Yes, please!" Little Nelly said. "We
can all be zoo mice!"

Just then, Micky came running.

"Look, Little Nelly! Look what I found out from your book!"

"What is it?" asked Little Nelly.

"I discovered that I'm not a mouse after all!" said Micky.

"Really? Then what are you?" said Little Nelly.

"I'm **an elephant!**" said Micky.

Elephants can be:
brown
gray ✓

Elephants have
big ears. ✓

Elephants have
skinny tails. ✓

"That's interesting," said Little Nelly. "But, Micky, even though you aren't a mouse like me, I'll still be your friend."

"Thanks, Little Nelly!" said Micky.

Which just goes to show why books should **always** have pictures.